What do the grown-ups do?

Joe the Fisherman

"Utterly charming, full of facts and a great career guide."
Tony Boullemier, author of The Little Book of Monarchs.

"An informative and fun way to introduce your children to the world of living."
Gordon Buchanan, Wildlife film maker
(BBC Springwatch, Autumnwatch, The Polar Bear Family and Me).

"What a refreshing and innovative way of introducing children to career possibilities in later life. A delightful series of books which gently guides younger children through the adult world of work. The accompanying photographs of the main characters bring the lives of Joe the Fisherman, Fiona the Doctor and Papa the Stock Farmer, to life."
Louise White, Broadcaster.

"Really detailed and informative books, which contain exactly the questions that intelligent children ask, and adults are often unable to answer. There is fun, humour and a wonderful sense of place too."
Dr Ken Greig, Rector, Hutchesons' Grammar School.

"As an educator in the US there is more and more stress placed upon children being able to access non-fiction writing. Within her books, Mairi McLellan has done something many children's authors are unable to do: she has created non-fiction books that are compelling and highly readable. May all of children's non-fiction literature begin to engage students as McLellan's books do. If this is a new trend in children's books, teachers across the US would be so grateful."
Marlene Moyer, 5th & 6th Grade teacher, Nevada, USA.

Matador
9 Priory Business Park
Kibworth Beauchamp
Leicestershire LE8 0RX, UK
Tel: (+44) 116 279 2299
Fax: (+44) 116 279 2277
Email: books@troubador.co.uk
Web: www.troubador.co.uk/matador

ISBN: 978 1783060 962

British Library Cataloguing in Publication Data.
A catalogue record for this book is available from the British Library.

Matador is an imprint of Troubador Publishing Ltd

www.kidseducationalbooks.com

What do the grown-ups do?

Joe the Fisherman

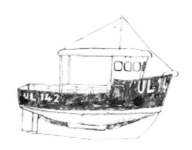

Mairi McLellan

What do the grown-ups do?

Dear reader,

What do the grown-ups do? is a series of books designed to educate children about the workplace in a light-hearted and interesting manner. The ideal age range is five to ten years and the feedback from the children has been superb. They seem to have a genuine interest in learning about the workplace, keen to understand what the grown-ups do all day.

The objective is to offer the children an insight into adult working life, to stimulate their thinking and to help motivate them to learn more about the jobs that interest them. Perhaps by introducing these concepts early, we can broaden their ideas for the future as well as increase their awareness of the world around them. It's just a start and at this age, although the message is serious, it is designed to be fun.

For younger children who will be doing a combination of reading and 'being read to', this book will be reasonably challenging. I have deliberately tried not to over-simplify the books too much to maintain reality, whilst making them fun to enjoy.

You can read the books in any order but they are probably best starting from the beginning. The order of the series can be found at the back of this book.

Many more will be coming soon so please check the website for updates www.kidseducationalbooks.com.

I hope you enjoy them.

Happy reading,

Mairi

A note of thanks to my wonderful family – Mum, Dad, Fiona, Neil, Ewan and my gorgeous girls. Also to my lovely extended McLellan family and of course to 'Joe' and co. at Macduff Peninsula.
Viva Badaneel.

Life by the sea in Badaneel

The Mackenzie girls lived by the sea in a pretty little village in the northwest Highlands called Badaneel. With big sandy beaches, tall mountains and wooded glens, it was one of the most beautiful places in Scotland.

Views around Badaneel.

Badaneel had a fantastic natural harbour, which was very sheltered with lots of boats moored in the bay. It was a great place to go sailing and watch the seals sunbathing on the rocks.

Seals on the rocks.

The village had little white houses around the bay and a café overlooking the sea. If the girls were good and had done their jobs at home, they were allowed to go to the café because it sold juice and crisps. It was always a great treat. They would sit on the stools, order their juice and crisps and then go and play outside by the water with their friends from the village.

Sometimes, if it was nice weather, they would all jump off the jetty into the Badaneel River. It was often a competition to see who could jump from the highest point and the current record holder was Christopher. Christopher was eleven years old and he was very brave.

The jetty by the café.

The girls were almost all the same age. The twins, Ava and Skye, were five and Gracie was only just over a year younger at four years old. Most people thought they were triplets because Gracie was tall for her age and managed to keep up very well with her older sisters. Everyone got them muddled up but they answered to any name!

The Mackenzie girls walking in the heather.

The girls spent a lot of time wandering around the hills amongst the heather. The views were fantastic. They liked to find a stick to help them because sometimes the heather grew taller than them!

Skye on the paddle-board.

The Mackenzie girls on the paddle-board.

In the summer they spent most of their time by the sea. They went sailing in their little sailing dinghy called *Puffin*, they jumped off the jetty by the pier, went out paddle-boarding, played football on the beach or rowed about in the rubber dinghy, pushing each other off into the water. It was great fun.

They were all good swimmers even though they were still quite young. However, every time they went on a boat they had to wear their lifejackets. Papa said that even if you were a good swimmer, you must wear a lifejacket. He said that even the best swimmers can't swim for long in the sea before getting too tired.

Most of the time they also wore wetsuits so they could stay in the cold water for longer. The wetsuits helped them float and keep warm so they could play for hours!

Jobs

However, the girls also had jobs to do. Their parents said that everyone had to work and the girls were good workers. They earned pocket money to buy juice and crisps at the café or a new football. Their aunt's dog had chewed seven footballs this year so it was quite expensive to keep replacing them! Their jobs included:

- Fishing and lifting lobster pots
- Getting logs for the fire
- Tidying their room
- Vacuum cleaning
- Sweeping the front steps
- Watering the vegetables in the garden
- Doing the dishes
- Planting flowers
- Washing down paintwork
- Peeling vegetables
- and many more …

Their parents gave them pocket money for their work and whilst they enjoyed it, they were generally rather more interested in what the grown-ups were doing.

They didn't quite understand why grown-ups always had to work so much. It wasn't just their parents, it was all parents. It also seemed that the grown-ups had more money for their work and this was all very confusing.

Ava, Skye and Gracie were interested in finding out more about the grown-up work and decided to approach Mother about the matter.

"We would like to see what the grown-ups do, Mama. Can you show us please?" asked Ava.

"Well," said Mother, "there are so many jobs out there. There are literally thousands of different jobs."

"How do you know which job to do?" asked Skye.

"I suppose you need to try to understand a little about the jobs that interest you and make a decision from there," said Mother. "The most important thing to do is find something that you enjoy doing. There is no point in doing a job that just earns lots of money if you are going to be miserable whilst doing it. Working takes up more than half of your life and so it is important to be happy at your work.

Having said that, you have to find a job that pays you enough to be able to keep up with whatever standard of living you are happy with. It's a bit of a balance."

"We like sailing and jumping off the jetty, Mama!" said Gracie. "Can we get a job doing that?"

"It's not quite so simple, Gracie!" laughed Mother. "Yes, there are jobs in sailing, for example, teaching sailing, delivering yachts for people, cleaning and cooking on big boats and so on. However, I suspect there are not many jobs that will pay you to jump off a jetty. That's known as *play* rather than work! Would you like to go and see some grown-ups working?" asked Mother.

Approach to Badaneel bay from the East.

"Yaaaaay!" screamed the children. "We want to go to work with the grown-ups!"

"OK, everyone," said Mother. "I'll have a chat with some people to see what you can learn about grown-up jobs. Is there a particular job that you would like to start with?"

"Hmmmm," mumbled the girls, looking at each other for inspiration. "We like being in the sea, Mama," said Gracie. "Can we get a job that is in the sea?"

"I'd say that's a good start, Gracie," said Mother. "Why don't we ask Joe the Fisherman if he'll show us his work and maybe he'll explain it all to us."

"Yaaaaay! Joe the Fisherman. We like Joe!" they shouted.

Macduff Peninsula

The following weekend, they headed over to Macduff Peninsula where the Macduff family had lived and worked on the fishing boats for generations. They were a lovely family and great neighbours.

Ava, Skye and Gracie knew Joe and his brother Jack well. Sometimes their parents went down the road to Macduff Peninsula with the wheelbarrow and came back with a barrow-full of prawns to eat for dinner.

Their mother cooked the prawns in a huge pot on the stove. It was enormous and was used for feeding lots of people. Mother called it the 'witches cauldron' because it was so big! The prawns were boiled in the cauldron for a few minutes and then they all sat at the big table to eat them with garlic butter. They were delicious!

Joe and Jack splicing rope.

Joe the Fisherman

Joe was a great strong man, standing over six foot tall with broad shoulders and a big wide grin. He was always happy and constantly telling stories and jokes. He often let the kids try to wrestle him and the three of them would jump all over him. Occasionally he would let them win but they knew he was just pretending. Joe had been fishing since he was a boy, just as his father before him.

Joe mending creels.

The fishing boat arriving home.

"Good morning girls!" he shouted over from the pier. "Have you come to help me today?"

"Joe! Hi Joe! Mama said we could come and see what jobs the grown-ups do and we want to be fishermen today! Can you show us please?"

Joe was busy mending creels. He said it was penance for not being at sea. Today was really windy with forty knots of wind and it was not good for going out in the boat. Joe said the creels would bounce up and down and get damaged in this kind of weather. He also said that *he* would bounce up and down and get damaged! Besides, there was plenty of work to be getting on with, mending and cleaning the creels.

"There are lots of types of fishing," said Joe. "Being a fisherman is quite a general term because there are lots of different fish and shellfish and there are lots of different ways to catch them. There is trawling, long line fishing, jigging, scallop dredging and creel fishing to name a few."

"What type of fisherman are you Joe?" asked Ava.

"I am a creel fisherman. I catch prawns in my lobster pots or 'creels'. We go out every day at 6am in the creel boat. It takes us about three quarters of an hour to travel to our pots where we lift the creels and put other ones down. We use different areas but we have our favourite spots. Depending on the day, we return home around 4-5pm."

A prawn just off the boat.

"What are your favourite parts of your job?" asked Skye.

"I love it when we get calm, sunny days especially when we catch lots of prawns. My brother and I get to see amazing sunrises, which are always a treat.

We love seeing dolphins and some days we have literally thousands around the boat, jumping in the bow wave. Even in winter we can have lovely days, watching the sun setting down behind the mountains of the Western Isles.

We also get a little bit of pleasure when we hear the radio talking about some poor guy stuck in a thirty-two mile traffic jam on the motorway down south, although I couldn't really say that was a favourite part of the job!

I just love being out on the water on sunny days with the lovely scenery, sunsets and dolphins."

Dolphin jumping near Badaneel.

The *Mo-Rùn* (mo-roon) – Joe's father's old fishing boat on a stormy day.

"What is the worst part of your job?" asked Ava.

"Definitely bad weather. When the day starts with bad weather you know you are going to get a beating from dawn until dusk. It's rarely a good day! I also don't like it when we don't catch many prawns. Just to complicate matters, we often struggle to catch prawns on a calm day because they need oxygen in the water to thrive.

On a calm day they rush off to shallower water to find oxygenated water. This means that sometimes we don't catch many prawns on calm days, which makes it a bad day for business, but a pleasant day at sea! "

"How do you catch the prawns?" asked Gracie.

Joe got out a pen and drew them a diagram. "It's a little difficult to explain so I'll draw you a picture.

We have a long line of rope that sinks in the water between two brightly coloured buoys. We put eighty creels on one long line and they sink to the bottom of the sea where the prawns live. We have to have the right spacing or it won't work properly. It's a bit like this." He drew two buoys in a line with ropes hanging from them.

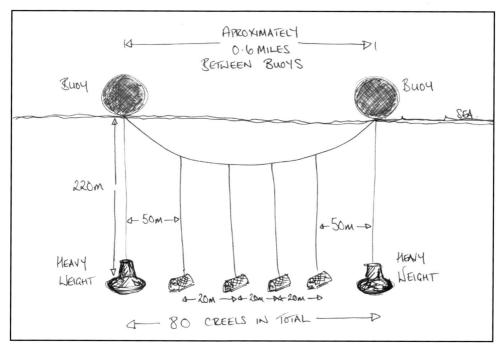

Drawing of how to lay the creels.

"The line sinks with the weight of the creels. The top line needs to sink right down otherwise it will catch on the propellers of boats going by."

The creels out on the water near Badaneel.

Joe then explained that they needed to put something tasty inside the creels so that the prawns wanted to go in. "We put herring bait inside the creels to attract the prawns. We used to catch the herring but there are hardly any herring left here anymore. Nowadays we buy frozen herring, de-frost it and put it in a barrel mixed with just the right amount of salt."

Barrels used to store the herring bait.

"How much salt do you put in?" asked Skye.

"Oh then! That would be telling! It's a secret recipe!" laughed Joe. "What I can tell you is that prawns and fish like fresh bait, whereas lobsters like really smelly bait. You have to leave the lobster bait until it is all brown and stinky and until it has a thick brown oil on top. The lobsters love that!"

"Yuk!! " cried the children. "Imagine eating rotten fish!"

"You'd be surprised what they eat," chuckled Joe. "Did you know that lobsters can't eat meat because it makes the lobster poisonous?"

"No, we didn't know," they mumbled. "We'll tell Daddy. We use fish for bait in our lobster pots at home, but we are always catching crabs. Maybe that's because we are not leaving the fish to get really smelly?"

"That will be it!" laughed Joe. "The smellier the better for lobster!"

The herring bait just right for prawns, brown oil on the top and fresh underneath.

"Do you have to be very strong to be a fisherman?" asked Ava.

"Not necessarily, although you need to be strong when things go wrong, which at some point they will! However, my mother used to fish with my father, so not everyone on the boat needs to be really strong, but it definitely helps."

Joe lifting creels from the boat.

"How do you become a fisherman? Can anyone start fishing?" asked Skye.

"Ideally you need to be taught by someone on the boat. In this particular line of work, there is nothing better than learning on the job. Fishing is not a job for everyone – it's better if you enjoy being at sea and don't get seasick!

The job can be really dangerous in bad weather and you need to have special qualifications in sea survival, fire fighting and first aid to even get on the boat to work. These can all be done.

One of the hardest parts is saving enough money to buy the boat and creels. These days, the banks don't often give you money to buy a boat, so it is really difficult to start out on your own and you have to save up all your pocket money!"

"How do you make money from your fishing?" asked Gracie.

"There is a company that buys our prawns. They come here a couple of times each week to take the prawns to the city to be packaged up. From there they go to London, France and Spain to be sold. We make money because people want to eat our prawns and they pay money to buy them."

A tube of prawns.

Stacks of tubes ready for collection.

The tubes are loaded into the van.

"What happens if all the prawns get caught and there are no more to fish?" asked Gracie.

"Now that is a very good question," laughed Joe, "with no easy answer! This is a big debate at the moment. Not so long ago there used to be tonnes of fish swimming around the sea. Today there are hardly any by comparison.

The main cause is 'over-fishing'. That means that we are catching fish (or shellfish) faster than nature can replace the supply. As a result, year after year, there are fewer fish in the sea. Over generations, fishing has become increasingly efficient and we have bigger boats working more effectively to catch the fish.

Some types of fishing are more damaging than others. There are lots of ideas on how to improve the situation but there is no simple fix to the problem."

"Why don't they just stop people fishing so much?" asked Gracie.

"It's not that easy, Gracie. Over one billion people in the world rely on fish as their main source of protein. This means that if an area is 'over-fished' there is a food shortage for a lot of people!

The people who work on the fishing boats depend on this for a living. In other words, they need this work to earn money to feed their families – little boys and girls like you.

Many of them work really hard, going to sea for seven to fourteen days at a time, working on what is basically a moving processing factory. It's a hard life," explained Joe.

"So what can be done to stop all the fish dying?" persisted Gracie.

"Some people have suggested the creation of a 'no-fishing' zone to allow a few years for the fish stock to rebuild. This is a good long term idea but in reality it is difficult if it means that a parent cannot put food on the family table!

It is a difficult problem to solve. The cost of fuel is so high that ultimately what may happen is that the big trawlers will not make any money due to the high diesel costs, so they will have to find some other type of work. It is also possible that the big boats may increase their 'mesh size', that is the hole size in the nets. This means that the smaller fish don't get stuck in the net so they can grow to become adults, but no-one really knows what to do or when a solution will be found."

Sustainable Fishing

"My brother Jack and I, as well as many locals here, work differently," said Joe. "Our kind of creel fishing has been described by Greenpeace as 'the most ecologically friendly commercial fishing in the world! How's that girls!

We work on what we call a 'sustainable fishing system'. By that I mean we put back all the smaller prawns and keep only the big ones. We have a special small hole in our creels called an 'escape hole' so that the small ones can get out.

Creels with little blue escape holes for the smaller prawns to get out.

The size of the prawns that go back!

When the creels are landed in the boat, we sort them all out by hand and if the small ones come into the boat, we throw them back into the sea so they can grow to become adults.

If they are smaller than this," and he held up his hand to show them, "then they go back. We also throw back all the 'berried females', which are females that are going to have babies.

By doing this, we are helping to protect the prawns for the future. Most, but not all of the creel fishermen here from Point Beach to Plumcross, fish using sustainable creel fishing. The trouble is that many parts of the country do not and so the problem persists."

Jack shows us the size that the prawns should be.

"Are there still going to be prawns to fish when we are grown-up?" asked Ava.

"Yes, darling, I think so. The future is not clear but I am hopeful that something will be done to protect fishing. It is likely to involve a combination of increasing the mesh size, protecting areas for re-generation and generally adopting a more sustainable approach!

The public also wants a better product which is fresh and not damaged. This is all good news for creel fishing. We catch them in an eco-friendly manner, we use less fuel because we often just work at tick-over speed and we get a higher price for our product because it is of a high quality. All of this means it should still be a good job by the time you are grown-up."

Ava, Skye and Gracie thought this all sounded rather complicated but they kind of understood.

"OK," said Ava. "So you have to fish properly or all the fish will die. You also have to like the sea and it's best not to be seasick. You need to have a proper boat and learn from someone who knows, in order to be a fisherman. You have a good day if it's nice and calm but then you might not catch enough fish because they don't have enough air, and when it's too windy to go to sea you work on the pier cleaning and mending. Is that right?"

"Absolutely my dear," replied Joe, "you girls have been listening well!"

Creels at Badaneel pier.

"Why do you have to clean the creels if they are in the water anyway?" asked Gracie.

"Ah, you see, even though they are in the water, they get all covered in slime eventually. Every six to seven months we have to clean them because the prawns won't go inside them or even near them if they are dirty! We take them ashore to wash, repair and swap them over with spare ones. We are always working on the creels. There is never any time to be bored. Are you girls ever bored?" he asked.

"No! Mama says that only stupid people get bored. She says there is always something to either work on or play with."

Joe laughed. "Absolutely right! Living in the country is never boring and if you get a spare moment there are always logs to cut, gardening to do or, as you can see, creels to mend! And on that note, I shall have to get back to work girls. Has this been helpful? Do you know more about creel fishing now?"

"Oh yes!" cheered the girls. "We are going to go home and tell Mama all about it. We are also going to tell Daddy that we need to leave that lobster bait in the barrel for longer until it is really smelly. That way we might stop catching crabs inside our lobster pots!"

"Glad to be of help girls. Come over and chat again soon. Maybe next time, I'll show you how to splice the ropes?" smiled Joe.

"Thanks Joe!" they shouted and off they went, running back up the track to their house, chattering about being fishermen. When they got back to the house, they had a cup of hot chocolate and told their mother all about their chat with Joe. They really liked Joe the Fisherman, he was a great guy and they had learned a lot about creel fishing.

However, Ava wasn't so sure the job was for her. "I get seasick Mama and I don't think that would be very good for being a fisherman. Can we look at some other jobs?" she asked.

"Indeed Ava, how right you are," smiled Mother. "Seasickness and fishing jobs do not go very well together! Besides, you can't make a decision on what you want to do until you have seen lots of different jobs. Let's look and see what other jobs we can find..."

 # The end.

Next stop: Papa the Stock Farmer.